Little Frankie at His Plays

Madeline Leslie

Copyright © 2023 Culturea Editions
Text and cover : © public domain
Edition : Culturea (Hérault, 34)
Contact : infos@culturea.fr
Print in Germany by Books on Demand
Design and layout : Derek Murphy
Layout : Reedsy (https://reedsy.com/)
ISBN : 9791041819614
Légal deposit : July 2023

LITTLE FRANKIE AT HIS PLAYS

CHAPTER I

FRANKIE AND HIS WHEELBARROW.

I HAVE already told you that Frankie lived in a pretty cottage, separated from the road by a green lawn, which lay in front of it. On the other side of the street, the land was much lower, a little shining brook running through it, and sometimes, after a rain, there was quite a pond of water. In winter this was a pleasant place for Willie to skate. His mamma liked it, because she could watch him from the windows; Willie liked it, because when his hands were cold he could run home to warm himself; and Frankie liked it, because it made him laugh and clap his hands to see his brother bow and turn this way and that, run a few steps, and then make such pretty figures on the ice. He had no doubt at all but Willie did all this just to amuse him. If you could have seen him as he stood in his chair at the front window, how he jumped up and down, and threw his head back, and then held it far forward on his breast, laughing so merrily, bursting out afresh every time Willie made a bow or stretched out his arms, you could not have helped laughing yourself, out of sympathy.

Sally seemed to enjoy it as much as he did.

"I declare," she said one day, as her mistress entered the room and found her sitting by the fire with her work, while Frankie stood at the window, "I haven't laughed so much in a month. It does one's heart good just to see how the little fellow enjoys his brother's sport."

Back of the house where he lived there was a barn. His papa did not keep a horse in it, but one day, after some months, a gentleman came to pass a few days at the cottage, and his horse was put up in the barn. One pleasant evening, when papa, and mamma, and their friends were walking in the garden, the gentleman said he would lead his horse down to the pond, and give him some water to drink, and he invited Willie to ride upon the horse's back. Willie's papa helped him on, and he held fast by the horse's mane. When he came back, Frankie wanted to ride too. Mamma was afraid he would fall; but the gentleman said the horse was gentle, and papa said he would hold him very tightly.

So Frankie mounted the horse, and took his first lesson in riding. Papa was going to walk about the grounds, but the little boy said, "Pony want water gen, papa; pony must have more water."

Frankie had never been to the pond before. First they had to cross the road, then go through the rail fence into the field. The gentleman let down two bars, and the horse carefully stepped over the other. Then papa held his baby very tight, because they were going down a steep place into the water. The gentleman thought pony would not drink again; but he did, and Frankie leaned over, and saw him suck up great mouthfuls of water. Then they turned back, and went out of the field, papa holding the horse, while the gentleman put up the bars again.

Mamma was very glad to get her boy safely home. She had been anxious all the time, for fear he would fall and hurt himself, though papa laughed, and told her there was no danger. She had kept Ponto near her, for fear he would bark and frighten the strange horse. But the moment Frankie was taken off, he flew up to him, and licked his face and hands, and tried to spring on his neck, he was so glad to see him.

I don't know what Frankie would have done without Ponto. Willie and Margie were at school; and there were a great many hours when he would have had to play alone. But Ponto was always ready for a frolic. He was never tired or out of humor, though sometimes he was rather too rough; and then he loved his young master so much, that he wanted to kiss him oftener than Frankie liked.

Early in the summer, papa had bought a wheelbarrow for his boy to roll in the yard. It was painted red, and on the sides were pretty pictures painted in gilt. It had long, smooth handles, and a large wheel, so that it ran along the walks very nicely indeed.

I wish you could have been there to see what pleasant plays Frankie had with his dog and his wheelbarrow; but as you were not, I will try to tell you about it.

Mamma had made a pretty sun bonnet, with a deep frill to shade his face, and as soon as the sun had dried up the dew, she tied it on his head, and let him run all about the grounds with only Ponto to take care of him.

Ponto knew very well that the little fellow was left in his charge; and when mamma said, "Ponto, look here, sir; take care of your little master," he would hold up his head, and wag his tail, and bow, wow, wow, as much as to say, "Yes, indeed, ma'am."

Then Frankie would run along wheeling his barrow, and Ponto close beside him, until they came to the woodpile. Here the little boy stopped, and began to fill his barrow with sticks; and Ponto picked them up in his teeth almost as fast as Frankie did with his hands. Sometimes he was wild and full of fun, so that when Frankie wanted to take the stick from his mouth and put it in the barrow, Ponto would spring up into the air, and run away; but when he heard his master say, "Come here, sir," he would be sober in a moment. O, Ponto was a very knowing dog indeed!

When the barrow was full, Frankie rolled it to the back door, and put it in a basket set there for him by Jane. When she saw him coming, she called out through the window, "Sure and he's not a baby at all, but a man entirely, to be bringing me all my wood. Sure and I'll make him a nice cake for his supper."

Then Frankie felt very large, and walked off with his head up and his lips parted in a pleasant smile.

By and by Frankie would be tired of wheeling wood; then he used to take Jane's small kitchen shovel, and fill his barrow with sand; and what do you think he did with it. I am sure you cannot guess. Why, he poured it all over Ponto. The first time he did this, the dog did not like it at all; but when he heard Frankie laughing so merrily, and saw how much he was pleased, he felt, I suppose, willing to submit. So he lay down again in the walk, and this time Frankie laughed so that he did not half fill the barrow before he poured it over the dog again.

Much as he tried to like it, I suppose Ponto was not very much pleased, for he soon got up and shook himself thoroughly, and then barked a little, as if to say, "No more, if you please."

CHAPTER II.

FRANKIE AND HIS DOG.

A FEW days after Frankie's ride on horseback, he was out of doors playing with Ponto, and he thought he would take a walk down to the pond. Before this time, he had been a very good boy, and had never gone through the gate into the road, though sometimes he would stand at the fence, and look through to see people passing by.

Mamma was busy in the parlor with company; and Sally was at work in the back part of the house.

When Ponto saw that his master was going into the street, he began to bark furiously, for he knew this was not exactly right. Mrs. Gray heard him, and ran to the window; but just at this moment Frankie was behind a tree, and she did not see him; so she thought that the dog was barking at something he saw in the road.

For a minute Ponto was very much excited, and ran back toward the house, but presently turned and followed Frankie to the water.

The little boy did not seem at all afraid, but went right down the steep path where he had rode on the horse. I suppose he thought the water looked very pretty, for he walked right into it up to his waist.

A few minutes after Frankie went away from the back door, Sally went out to shake the hearth rug. As she did not see him any where about, she called, "Frankie, Frankie! Ponto, Ponto!" She ran around to the front of the house, still calling, "Frankie, Frankie!" and "Ponto, Ponto!"

Mamma heard her, and ran to the door.

"Have you seen Frankie, ma'am?" asked Sally, pale with fright.

"Where's Ponto?" cried the lady, without stopping to answer.

"There he is," screamed nurse, running as fast as she could toward the water.

Mamma ran too, and the ladies who were in the parlor; but mamma was so frightened that her head swam round and round, and she could hardly stand.

When Ponto heard them coming, he barked louder than ever, but he did not run toward them; and Sally sprang over the fence without waiting to let the bars down, and in one moment more caught the poor frightened Frankie in her arms. Ponto had taken the little fellow in his teeth, and put him on the bank.

He lay quite still, as if he were very tired, only when Sally placed him in his mamma's arms, he put up his little wet hand, and tried to stroke her cheek. His eyes were very red, as if he had been crying, and his clothes all dripping with water and stained with mud. Sally ran forward to get the bath tub filled with warm water, while mamma carried him gently toward the house.

No one seemed to be in such good spirits as Ponto. He danced and jumped, trying to catch Frankie's foot, and whisked his tail up and down, and did every thing he could to express his joy at having his little friend safe again.

How and when the ladies went away mamma did not know. She carried her dear boy up into the nursery, and then sank down, and began to cry. When Sally saw her, she cried too; and Jane, who, was pulling off Frankie's stockings, wiped her eyes with her apron. They were all crying for joy that dear, darling little Frankie had not been drowned. And mamma whispered a few words as she bent over her boy. She knew that God could hear, and so she said, "O my heavenly Father, I do thank thee for restoring my precious child to my arms. Once more I give him to thee."

While she was washing him, she told Sally that she had heard Ponto bark some time before, but could not see that Frankie was with him. "I shall always love Ponto," she said, "for he saved my boy."

Ponto was lying on the hearth rug, resting himself. He had had a great deal to do that morning, and he had done it well. Now, when he heard mamma repeat his name, he rapped with his tail on the floor.

"Good fellow!" said mamma; "good Ponto!"

He rapped again, louder than before. This was the way he meant to say, "I am as glad as you are, that dear Frankie is safe."

When the little fellow had been dressed in his clean clothes, Sally said she would run down to the water and bring up his wheelbarrow, which she saw there. Jane went with her, and they found where he went in, for his tiny shoe was sticking fast in the mud. Then they went round to the other side, where Ponto had carried him, and found it was very deep water, so that if the noble dog had not taken him out, he must have been drowned.

When Willie came home from school, and heard what a trusty friend Ponto had been, he put his arms round the dog's neck and kissed him. Frankie had kissed him very often, but Willie had never done so before. But Ponto seemed to understand it very well; and when papa came in, all the while mamma was telling him about poor Frankie's accident, he stood gazing into her face.

For a few moments papa could not speak; his heart was too full. He walked away to the window and wiped his eyes; but presently he came back, and patted Ponto on the head, and said, "Noble Ponto! good fellow!"

Then Ponto knew that he was glad too; and he went to the bed where Frankie was lying, and putting up his fore paws, began to lick the little fellow's hand.

When Sally took up the wet clothes to carry them to the wash, there were the marks of Ponto's teeth, where he had fastened them firmly through the dress, cambric and flannel skirts.

CHAPTER III.

FRANKIE IN TRIAL.

I HAVE told you so much about Frankie, I suppose you will want to know whether he was always a good boy. Did he never show a naughty temper? Was he never unkind to his brother Willie? or to his little nurse Margie? Did he never tell a lie? never take what was not his own? I am sorry to say that he did some of these things, and no doubt would have done a great many more, but that he had a kind mamma and papa to teach him.

One of the greatest blessings which God can give a little boy or a little girl, is a good Christian mother. I hope, my dear young friend, if God has been so kind as to give you such a mother, that you will thank him every day of your life.

When you wake up in the morning and repeat your little hymn, thanking God for letting you see another day, with the pleasant sun and sweet-smelling flowers, don't forget to thank him, too, for giving you a dear mamma to love you and watch over you.

And then, when you are tired with play, and lie down at night to rest your head upon the soft pillow, don't go to sleep without thanking him for preserving her who has prepared you nice food, made you warm clothes, and tried to lead your little feet in the path of right.

I think whatever faults little Frankie had, he dearly loved his mother. Ever so many times in a day he would run to her side, sometimes right in the midst of his play, and say, "I want to kiss oo. I love oo."

When he meddled with her work-basket, or did other troublesome things, and she spoke sharply, "Frankie, don't do so," he would turn in a moment and ask, with a quivering lip, "Am I your darling now, mamma?"

Once in a while Frankie would get up in the morning, and instead of the bright smile he generally wore, his face looked cross. Nurse used to say he got out of bed the wrong way. When this was the case, nothing seemed to go right with him. At breakfast he pushed away his plate, and would not let Margie fasten on his bib, and seemed very unhappy. This was not because he was sick, but because he was out of humor, and needed to be brought right again.

His mamma was very much troubled about it, and she said to herself, "If I do not correct my little son, he will grow more unhappy, and his temper will become so sullen that no one will love him; and what is worst of all, God will not love him." She went away alone into her chamber, and knelt down by her bed, and asked God to direct her what to do in order to make Frankie a good boy.

I suppose God did put some good thoughts into her mind, for the next day, when the little boy was naughty again, she arose at once, and led him away to her chamber, and talked with him a long time. And then they knelt down together, and she held his little hands while she asked God to take away his wicked heart, and give him a good one, that would be full of pleasant, happy thoughts, and of love to the dear Saviour and to every body.

Perhaps you would like to know one thing she told him. It was this. She said, "My dear Frankie, when you look so cross, and speak unkindly to Willie, and do not wish to obey me, do you know who is close by you, whispering in your ear?"

"No, mamma," said Frankie; "I didn't see any body."

"It is the wicked Satan," said mamma. "He likes to see you naughty, and so he puts unkind thoughts into your heart. He would like to have you naughty all the time, because then he knows you could not be happy. He don't like good children, and he can't bear to stay where they are; so he has to run off by himself when you are obedient, and kind, and happy. Shall I tell you what I think he was whispering in your ear this morning?"

"Yes, mamma."

"Well, when you rubbed out Willie's figures, after he asked you not to do so, I think he said, 'I wouldn't mind my brother; I'd do it just to vex him.' Then, when I forbade you to touch it again, he whispered, 'Get away, mamma; I don't love you this morning.'"

Frankie hung down his head, and looked very sober. He did not like to think he had been pleasing Satan, but still he was troubled, for he did not know exactly what to do. In a minute he said, "I will try to be good Frankie, mamma."

"That is right, my darling. If you try to be good, and when you hear Satan tempting you to do such wicked things, tell him at once to go away, then the good Spirit will come and help you to be kind, and to do every thing that is right. If you had not been listening to Satan this morning, you could have heard him, though he talks very softly indeed."

"What did he say, mamma?" asked Frankie.

"I suppose he was saying, 'Willie is a very kind brother, and loves you dearly. I wouldn't trouble him, my dear;' and then when I spoke, perhaps he said, 'Your mother knows what is right, little boy. She does it for your good, for she wants you to be happy.'"

CHAPTER IV.

FRANKIE'S BLOCK HOUSE.

A FEW days after mamma talked with Frankie, he was building a high house on the floor with his blocks, when Sally passed along and hit them, and over they went. The little boy looked very angry. "You naughty girl," he said.

Mamma laid down her work, and gazed at him, and her eyes looked very sorry. As soon as Sally went out of the room, she said, "What is Satan whispering to you now, my dear?"

Frankie started up and looked behind him: "I don't see him any where," he said.

"But didn't you hear his voice?" asked mamma.

"Yes, I did: he said, 'Throw a block at nurse; she is so naughty to knock your house over.'"

"Shall I blow Satan away?" said mamma.

"Yes, please."

She blew very hard; then opened the door, and blew again, as if she meant to send him off. "Now he's gone, I think," she said, looking in Frankie's bright face.

"The next time he comes I'll whip him, mamma," cried the little fellow, standing very straight, "'cause he tells me naughty things."

In a few minutes Sally came in again, and glanced at the little boy to see whether he felt happier than he did before.

Frankie looked at her, too, and his mamma thought he seemed sorry that he had called her naughty. She called him to her, and whispered, "Is any body speaking to you now, my darling?"

"Yes, mamma. It says, 'Tell Sally you're sorry.'"

"Are you going to mind the good Spirit?"

"Yes, mamma. I'm sorry, nurse, I called you naughty."

Nurse looked very much pleased. "I am sorry myself, dear," she said, "that my dress hit your blocks; and, if mamma is willing, I'll build you a high house."

"Yes, indeed," said mamma.

So Sally sat down on the carpet, and Frankie passed her the blocks; and she built a meeting house, with a high steeple. Mamma thought it was splendid, and the little boy danced about, and put his arms round Sally's neck, and kissed her ever so many times. "I'm so happy, mamma," he said, when she had gone.

"Children are always happy, my dear," she said, "when they have tried to be good."

"Satan can't stay here now; can he, mamma?"

"No, he has gone to trouble some other little boy with naughty thoughts."

The next morning, Frankie had forgotten all about this; and when papa said he must not have so much sugar on his cakes, his lips began to pout, and they were all afraid he was going to be very naughty.

Mamma leaned over her plate, and said, softly, "Is Satan here again?"

"Yes, mamma," said Frankie; "may I whip him out?"

She nodded yes; and he then jumped down from the table, and began to blow with all his might. Then he caught up a newspaper, and whisked it all about, saying, "Go long, old feller; go long out of this house."

"Whew! whew!" said papa; "what is all this?"

Mamma smiled, as if she understood it well; and presently the little fellow climbed up in his chair, looking very bright and happy, but quite out of breath with his exercise.

"Satan's gone, papa," he said. "Now I'm your dear little Frankie."

"Yes, indeed, you are," said his father, laughing heartily. "I am glad we have found a way to get rid of Satan so easily."

"What does it mean?" asked Willie.

"I will tell you presently, my dear," said papa.

When they had done breakfast, Mr. Gray opened the Bible for prayers, and taking Frankie on his knee, and calling Willie to stand by his side, he said, "In God's book, he tells us that Satan is our great enemy, who is trying to make us do wrong. He is called a roaring lion, who goeth about seeking whom he may devour. This means that he loves to destroy our happiness, and to see people miserable; and he knows if we are naughty, we shall suffer. He goes about whispering in the ears of little boys and girls, prompting them to mischief, persuading them to tell lies, to be disobedient and unkind. If children listen to his voice, they soon become like him; but if they say, 'Get thee behind me, Satan,' or drive him away, as Frankie did,the Holy Spirit will come and put good thoughts into their minds, and teach them, as the Bible says, what they ought to say and what they ought to do."

Papa then knelt down, and holding Frankie's little hand, prayed that he might always listen to the voice of the good Spirit, and be led by it to do all that is right.

CHAPTER V.

FRANKIE AND THE SUGAR.

ONE morning Mrs. Gray was finishing a piece of work which she wished to send away, when Frankie ran in from the dining hall, and asked, "Mamma, may I have some chucher?" He meant sugar, but he could not speak the word plainly.

"Where is the sugar that you want, my dear?" asked mamma.

"On the table," said Frankie. "Nurse is washing the dishes."

"Look in my face, darling," said mamma, "Did you take any sugar without my leave?"

Frankie looked up with his clear, truthful eyes, and said, "No, mamma, I didn't take any."

"Then go and get two large lumps, and bring them to me."

The little boy ran off, saying, "I will, mamma; I will get some."

Presently he returned with them; and she said, "Now, my dear, you shall have these, because you didn't take any without asking leave."

A few months before this time, Willie one day found Frankie in the store closet dipping up sugar with his hand from the barrel, and crowding it into his mouth. His whole face was covered with sugar, when Willie lifted him down from the chair, and led him to his mother.

When mamma had washed his hands and face, she took him in her lap, and told him it was very naughty to take mother's sugar without her permission. When he wanted sugar, or candy, or figs, he must always ask for them. Since that time she had not known him to touch any thing until he had first asked leave. Once she had left a paper of cough candy in her drawer for several days, and she knew he often went to this drawer on errands for her. She was coughing severely one afternoon, and said, "I really wish I had some candy."

"I will get you some," he said. "I saw some in the drawer;" and away he ran for it.

Mamma was so much pleased that he had not taken any, that she gave him a small paper of sugar plums. The cough candy was not good for him.

Ever since Frankie could remember, his mamma had told him the pretty stories in the Bible. The account of Adam and Eve in the garden; the sad death of good Abel, and the punishment of wicked Cain; the ark, and the dreadful flood; the stories of Joseph and his brethren, of Samuel and of Ruth, were as familiar to him as the names of the family circle. Indeed, the little boy seemed to connect the events of the Bible with every thing he saw.

One day a gentleman gave him a short cane. He had often seen Frankie play horse with his father's cane, and he thought it would please the child to have one of his own.

Frankie was very much delighted, and ran around the garden with it for several hours, Ponto following close at his heels, quite delighted with thenew sport. At last he came in, and, sitting down by his mamma, began to play with the string she had tied around the head of the cane. Then he looked very thoughtful for a minute, when he said, "I don't like that cane any more."

"Why don't you like it?" she asked, in surprise.

"Because it killed good Abel, you know."

"O, no," said mamma, with a laugh. "That Cain was a man, and not a stick."

The little fellow was once playing out near the barn, when he fell and cut his finger against a piece of glass. It bled very freely, so that mamma could not bind it up. She told Sally to bring a bowl of water, and held his poor finger in it. The water was soon red with the blood; and Frankie cried louder than ever. All at once he stopped, and said, "Mamma, it seems like the Red Sea. How could the Israelites get through so much blood?"

"That was not red with blood, my dear," said mamma. "It was only the name of the sea. There are the Red Sea, and the Black Sea, and the White Sea."

Frankie was very fond of cake, and would have liked to make his whole supper of it. But mamma knew it would make him sick. Sometimes, when he was in the kitchen, Jane gave him a piece; and one day his mother was very much pleased when he came running to her with a rich cake in his hand, fresh from the oven. "May I eat it, mamma?" he asked. "I didn't taste it without your leave."

Mamma broke off a small piece, and gave it to him, and then took him in her lap, and repeated a pretty little hymn she had learned when she was a child. I think you will like to hear it too.

"Mamma, do hear Eliza cry;
She wants a piece of cake I know;
She will not stir to school without;
Do give her some, and let her go."

"O, no, my dear; that will not do;
She has behaved extremely ill;
She pouts instead of minding me,
And tries to gain her stubborn will.

"This morning, when she had her milk,
She gave her spoon a sudden twirl,
And tipped it over on the floor;
O, she's a naughty, wicked girl!

"And now, forsooth, she cries for cake;
But that I surely shall refuse;
For children never should object
To eating what their parents choose.

"The pretty little girl who came
To sell the strawberries here to-day,
Would have been very glad to eat
What my Eliza threw away;—

"Because her parents are so poor
That they have neither milk nor meat;
But gruel and some Indian cake
Are all the children have to eat.

"They have four little girls and boys;
Mary's the oldest of the whole,
And hard enough she has to work,
To help her ma—poor little soul!

"As soon as strawberries are ripe,
She picks all day, and will not stop
To play or eat a single one,
Till she has filled her basket up.

"Then down she comes and sells them all,
And lays the money up at home,
To buy her stockings and her shoes,
To wear when freezing winter's come.

"For then she has to trudge away,
And gather wood through piles of snow,
To keep the little children warm,
When bites the frost, and cold winds blow.

"And then, when she comes home at night,
Hungry and tired, with cold benumbed,
How she would jump to find a bowl
Of bread and milk all nicely crumbed!

"But she, dear child, has no such thing;
Of gruel and the Indian cake,
Whether she chooses it or not,
Poor Mary must her supper make.

"Eliza, dear, will you behave
So ill again, another day?
Be cross and pert, and cry for cake,
And fling your breakfast all away?"

"Ah, never, never, dear mamma!
I'm sorry that I gave you pain;
Forgive me, and I never will
Be such a naughty girl again."

CHAPTER VI.

FRANKIE'S ROCKING HORSE.

WHEN Frankie was between three and four years old, there were a good many words he could not pronounce distinctly. He could not say kitchen, but called it chichen; and he called sugar chucher. He could not say sing, but said ting. His papa was afraid he never would be able to pronounce them; and he took a great deal of pains to have him try to say them over and over again. He used to take Frankie on his knee, and make him sound s-s-, and then say s-sing. But Frankie always said s-ting.

One day his mamma was passing through the back hall, and she saw her little boy kneeling in a chair by the table where Jane was making bread. He was talking very earnestly, and she stopped a moment to hear what he was saying.

He was giving Jane a lesson. "Now say knife," he began. So Jane said "knife."

"No, that not wight; you must say s- knife."

Jane laughed: "knife is right," she said.

"No, no!" he repeated; "papa say s- knife; so you must say it wight."

He thought it was as well to put s- on any other word as on sing.

He was very fond of playing school, and was quite happy when Willie and Margie would be his scholars. Dinah was always set up in her chair too, and another dolly whose name was Lily Gray. Frankie would set them all before him, and then ask, "Margie, who first man?"

"Adam."

"Now, you good girl, you may go wight to your seat. Willie, who first boy?"

"Cain."

"Yes, that's wight; now you be vely till, cause I shall peach." Then he would stand in his chair and preach very loud, spreading his arms, and always closing with a long amen.

Once, when he was kneeling with his father, he thought the prayer rather long, and putting up his face, he whispered, "Say amen, papa;—can't you say amen?"

Frankie was very happy one day when his mamma told him that his aunt and cousin were coming to make them a visit. He packed all his playthings in a trunk, to have them ready for the little baby, and then went round the house telling every body that Eddie was coming to see him.

The day before they were expected, a beautiful present came for Frankie from Mr. Wallace, the same kind gentleman who had given him the silver cup.

Can you guess what it was? It was not a cup and ball, nor a top, nor an iron hoop, but a rocking horse with a carriage fastened to it large enough for him to get in it. Then there was a place for the whip, and two pairs of reins for him to drive with.

At first, Frankie stood looking at it, his eyes growing larger and larger, until papa asked, "Well, Frankie, how do you like your new horse?"

"Is it for me, papa, for mine own telf?" exclaimed the little boy, clapping his hands and dancing up and down. "O, I'm to glad!" Then raising his eyes, he said, soberly, "Tank you, Dod. Tank you vely much indeed."

His mamma had taught him that all our blessings come from God; and the dear boy wished to thank him for this new favor.

I can hardly tell you how much pleased he was with his present. He could scarcely stop riding to eat his dinner; and then had to put up the horse in the corner of the room he called the stable, and tie him very tightly to a chair, for fear he would run away. Then, before his mother noticed what he was about, he slipped from his seat, and carried his silver cup of water to the pony, and held it to his mouth to drink.

"Pony hungry," he said, when she called him back. "Pony vely hungry indeed."

When Willie and Margie came from school, mamma watched her boy, to see whether he would be generous, and allow them to share in his rides.

"O, my!" called out Willie, "how pretty it is! Let me get in."

"Yet, you may," said Frankie, stepping out of the carriage. "Here, take Dinah too. Dinah wants to wide."

While Willie was whipping the horse to make him go as fast as he could, Frankie danced up and down, every now and then calling out, "Go long, pony, go long!"

In the mean time, Margie stood awaiting her turn, hardly daring to expect that Frankie would give up his new plaything to her. Mamma was looking on too, and was very happy when he said, "There, Willie, you must get out now, cause Margie wants to wide. Top a minute, Margie; I'll fix the reins for you," he cried; and he went to the pony's head, and patted him, and said, "Whoa, sir, whoa!" just like any gentleman.

The next day, when Eddie and his mamma came, Frankie seemed very happy to share his pleasure with his little cousin. They rode away together to visit other papas and mammas, but always came back at last to the stable in the corner of the room.

Can you tell what it was made Mrs. Gray so happy, when she looked at the pretty pony? It was because her darling boy had not been selfish with it, and tried to keep it all to himself, but had liked to see others riding in it, and enjoying it too. When little boys or girls are generous and kind, then look for smiles and kisses from their mammas.

CHAPTER VII.

THE TRY COMPANY.

"O MAMMA!" cried Willie, one day, running home from school in great haste, "the boys are going to have a little company; may I have a soldier cap and belong to it?"

Mrs. Gray sat busily at work, but she at once laid down her sewing in her lap, and thought a moment, and then she said, "I want you to belong to my company, my dear!"

"What company, mamma? Will they wear soldier caps, and jackets with red all down here, and stripes on their pantaloons?"

"Yes, they will be all dressed up with plumes and stars on their shoulders. It will be called the Try Company."

"May I have a cap too?" asked Frankie.

"Yes, any little boy may join who will agree to the rules."

"Rules, mamma," said Willie, "Do companies have rules?"

"O, yes, my dear! Soldiers always have to obey the captain; and if an enemy comes, to go and fight him."

"Shall we fight, then?" asked the boy in surprise.

"There will be one kind of fighting, my dear; but it will not be fighting with swords. You may ask all the little boys, who wish to form a company, up here after school this evening, and I will talk with them. Perhaps they will like to join my company."

Willie laughed quite heartily. "Yours, mamma! Shall you be the captain?"

"If they choose me I shall, my dear."

As soon as Willie had gone to school, Mrs. Gray began to cut long strips of colored paper and wind them into plumes. There was a very long waving one of yellow for the captain, and one of blue for the lieutenant, and twelve of pink for the soldiers. She did not think there would be more than fourteen at first. Then she cut sheets of paper, and taught Sally to form them into caps; and after they were done, she sewed the plumes on, and laid them all out on the table, which stood in the hall, so as to attract the notice of the boys when they came in from school.

Next she sent Sally to the attic for some strips of red and blue cloth. Of the red she made pretty stars to fasten on the shoulders, while nurse cut long smooth stripes to trim their jackets and pantaloons.

They had but just finished their work when a shout from Willie called mamma to the door, where she saw a company of boys awaiting her orders.

"Come in," she said, smiling at their bright, expectant faces; "come in, and we will form the company."

As they entered the hall they stopped short at sight of the beautifully plumed caps. "O mamma!" was all that Willie could say.

She led them into the dining hall, and then told them her plan. "I want to form a company of boys," she began. "It will be called the 'Try Company,' because every one belonging to it must learn to try to do things for himself. But first of all I must tell you the rules. No little boy can join my company unless he will promise not to use one naughty or vulgar word, not to tell a lie, and not to be unkind. If he has ever told lies, he must try to do so no more. Next he must try in his lessons. Sometimes the words are very long, and boys say, 'I can't learn them;' but my company will never say so.

"My boys will say, 'I'll try.' If the geography lesson is difficult, and you can't readily find the places on the maps, you will think of your pretty plumes, and say, 'I won't give up; I'll try again.'

"Then, when the sum is long, and it makes your head ache to add up four and ten and two and five, you won't mind that, but keep on trying until you succeed."

"Mother wants to know if my little brother can't join your company," asked a dear boy whose name was James; "but he don't learn sums; he is too small."

"O, yes, indeed!" said mamma; "Frankie has a cap like the rest, and your brother shall have one too, and a star on his shoulder."

"May I carry my drum?" eagerly asked Willie.

"Certainly, my dear; but wait a little. I have not told all the rules yet. My company must try, too, when they are at play. If James throws a ball, and hits John, he must *try* not to do so again. And if John feels a little angry, and thinks it very hard for James to hurt him, he must *try* to put all these naughty thoughts away, and call it an accident, and say 'I don't believe he meant to do it.' Then, if James or Willie wants to be captain, and the company choose another, James or Willie must *try* to be pleased and good humored about it."

"I thought you were to be captain, mother," cried Willie.

"I am afraid you would all laugh," said mamma, "to see me marching round at the head of such a troop of boys."

"We would *try* not to," exclaimed Willie, laughing.

Mrs. Gray laughed too; and then she said, "I want to see whether you understand about my rules; so I shall ask you a few questions. I once saw a boy sawing a stick of wood. It was a very large stick, and the saw went hard; the little fellow sat down and looked at it. 'It's too large,' said he; 'I can't get through it. I may as well give up first as last.' But presently he said, 'I'll try once more though;' and he started up, and sawed away, up and down, up and down, until the stick fell in two. Then the boy laughed and wiped his forehead, which was quite wet with perspiration, and said, 'There, I'm right glad I tried again. I never should have done it without trying.' Now tell me, could that little fellow be admitted into the Try Company?"

"Yes, ma'am, O, yes, ma'am!" answered all the boys.

"He ought to be the captain," said one.

Willie blushed, and held down his head.

"I knew another boy, who was winding some silk for his mother," said the lady. "He jerked it so much that it snarled badly. He pulled it, and twitched it, and made it worse than ever; and then he said; 'I can't do any thing with it.' When his mother came back for the silk, there it was upon the chair, so tangled up that she could not use it."

"He can't belong," called out the boys.

"I think you understand quite enough to form the company," said mamma. "Now I will put the vote. Would you all like to form a Try Company? If you would, you may hold up your hands."

Every small hand was quickly raised.

"And you promise to *try*, according to the rules?" said the lady.

Each little hand was raised again.

"Who is the oldest boy?" she asked.

"Sammy Lanman, ma'am."

"Then I advise you to let Sammy be the captain the first time, and then each of you take turns, until it comes down to little Frankie."

"May I run home for my brother?" asked James.

The lady stopped a moment to count the boys, and finding there were only twelve with Frankie, and that there would be caps enough for all, she said yes.

While he was gone, Willie ran to his play room for his drum, and Mrs. Gray dressed the Try Company in their new uniform, which did indeed look very fine. Then James came leading his little brother Walter; and when they were all dressed, their captain arranged them in order, and they then marched off down the yard, into the road, looking as happy as you please. Mamma and nurse stood at the door gazing after them, while Jane and Margie stood in the walk, shading their eyes and laughing heartily.

Poor Sammy, indeed, found that the office of captain was a most responsible one. His face grew very red as he perceived the younger members marching out of line, and a sharp word of rebuke rose to his lips, as little Frankie laughed aloud in his glee.

But suddenly he remembered that he had promised not to speak unkindly, and his heart beat fast as he said to himself, "Any body will know such little boys can't train very well the first time. At any rate, I'll try to keep my temper."